SO-BIM-304

FEB 2016

WITHDRAWN

PRO SPORTS
SUPERSTARS

Superstars
of the
BOSTON
CELTICS

by Annabelle T. Martin

AMICUS HIGH INTEREST ❖ AMICUS INK

Amicus High Interest and Amicus Ink
are imprints of Amicus
P.O. Box 1329, Mankato, MN 56002
www.amicuspublishing.us

Copyright © 2016. International copyright reserved
in all countries. No part of this book may be reproduced
in any form without written permission from the publisher.

Library of Congress Cataloging-in-Publication Data
Martin, Annabelle T.
  Superstars of the Boston Celtics / by Annabelle T. Martin.
      pages cm. -- (Pro Sports Superstars (NBA))
  Includes index.
  Audience: Grade: K to Grade 3.
  ISBN 978-1-60753-765-6 (library binding)
  ISBN 978-1-60753-864-6 (ebook)
  ISBN 978-1-68152-016-2 (paperback)
  1. Boston Celtics (Basketball team)--History--Juvenile literature. 2.
Basketball players--United States--Biography--Juvenile literature. I. Title.
  GV885.52.B67M27 2015
  796.323'640974461--dc23
                          2014044131

Photo Credits: Paul Sancya/AP Images, cover; Dick Raphael/NBAE/Getty
Images, 2, 8, 11, 15, 16, 22; Winslow Townson/AP Images, 4–5; Bettmann/
Corbis, 6; Steve Lipofsky/Corbis, 12–13; Rich Pedroncelli/AP Images, 18;
Charles Rex Arbogast/AP Images, 20–21

Produced for Amicus by The Peterson Publishing Company
and Red Line Editorial.

Designer Becky Daum
Printed in Malaysia

HC 10 9 8 7 6 5 4 3 2 1
PB 10 9 8 7 6 5 4 3 2 1

BRAZORIA COUNTY LIBRARY
ANGLETON   TEXAS

TABLE OF CONTENTS

MEET THE BOSTON CELTICS

The Boston Celtics started in 1946. They have won 17 **titles**. The team has had many stars. Here are some of the best.

BOB COUSY

Bob Cousy joined the team in 1950. He ran fast. He made great passes. Fans loved watching him. Cousy entered the **Basketball Hall of Fame** in 1970.

BILL RUSSELL

Bill Russell is a legend. He loved to play. Russell played strong defense. He **blocked** shots. Russell won 11 titles with Boston.

Russell played basketball in the Olympics. He won a gold medal in 1956.

JOHN HAVLICEK

John Havlicek never quit. He played great defense. He helped Boston win eight titles. The last was in 1976.

Havlicek played more games than any other Celtics player.

LARRY BIRD

Larry Bird joined the Celtics in 1979. Bird did it all. He scored. He passed. He **rebounded**. People called him Larry Legend.

Bird was named Rookie of the Year in 1979.

KEVIN MCHALE

Kevin McHale was a great scorer. He twisted and turned. He jumped and spun. McHale helped win three titles in the 1980s.

ROBERT PARISH

Robert Parish joined the Celtics the same year as Kevin McHale. That was 1980. The players made great teammates. Parish was tall and quick. He played good defense. He also sank shots.

PAUL PIERCE

Paul Pierce played 15 seasons in Boston. He could shoot from far away. Pierce scored many three-pointers. He helped win a title in 2008.

JARED SULLINGER

Jared Sullinger joined the team in 2012. He soon became a star. Sullinger is great at getting rebounds. He quickly moves to the right spot to grab the ball.

The Celtics have had many great superstars. Who will be next?

TEAM FAST FACTS

Founded: 1946

Home Arena: TD Garden in Boston, Massachusetts

Mascot: Lucky the Leprechaun

Leading Scorer: John Havlicek (26,395 points)

NBA Championships: 17 (1957, 1959, 1960, 1961, 1962, 1963, 1964, 1965, 1966, 1968, 1969, 1974, 1976, 1981, 1984, 1986, 2008)

Hall of Fame Players: 24, including Bob Cousy, Bill Russell, John Havlicek, Larry Bird, Kevin McHale, and Robert Parish

WORDS TO KNOW

Basketball Hall of Fame – a museum that honors the best basketball players ever

blocked – stopped another player's shot

rebounded – grabbed a ball that bounced away from the basket after a missed shot

Rookie of the Year – an award given to the best new player in the NBA

title – an NBA championship victory

LEARN MORE

Books

Birle, Pete. *Boston Celtics*. La Jolla, Calif.: MVP, 2014.

Caffrey, Scott. *The Story of the Boston Celtics*. Mankato, Minn.: Creative Education, 2011.

Websites

Boston Celtics—Official Site
http://www.nba.com/celtics
Check player stats and see videos of your favorite Celtics.

NBA Hoop Troop
http://www.nbahooptroop.com
Follow your favorite basketball teams. Learn more about today's superstars.

INDEX